W9-AKU-255

FOLKS CALL ME
APPLESEED JOHN

A Picture
Yearling Book

FOLKS CALL ME
APPLESEED JOHN

to Betty

Published by
Bantam Doubleday Dell Books for Young Readers
a division of
Bantam Doubleday Dell Publishing Group, Inc.
1540 Broadway
New York, New York 10036

If you purchased this book without a cover you should be aware that this book is stolen property. It was reported as "unsold and destroyed" to the publisher and neither the author nor the publisher has received any payment for this "stripped book."

Text and illustrations copyright © 1995 by Andrew Glass

All rights reserved. No part of this book may be reproduced or transmitted in any form or by any means, electronic or mechanical, including photocopying, recording, or by any information storage and retrieval system, without the written permission of the Publisher, except where permitted by law. For information address Doubleday Books for Young Readers, New York, New York 10036.

The trademarks Yearling® and Dell® are registered in the U.S. Patent and Trademark Office and in other countries.

Visit us on the Web!
www.bdd.com

Educators and librarians, visit the
BDD Teacher's Resource Center at
www.bdd.com/teachers

ISBN: 0-440-41466-0
Reprinted by arrangement with Doubleday Books for Young Readers
Printed in the United States of America
September 1998
10 9 8 7 6 5 4 3 2 1

The author wishes to acknowledge the following sources:

BOTKIN, B. A., Editor. *A Treasury of American Folklore.* New York: Crown Publishers, 1944.

LORANT, Stefan. *Pittsburgh: The Story of an American City.* Garden City: Doubleday and Company, 1964.

MILLER, Olive Beaupre. *Heroes, Outlaws & Funny Fellows of American Popular Tales.* New York: Cooper Square Publishers, 1973.

PRICE, Robert. *Johnny Appleseed: Man and Myth.* Gloucester: Peter Smith, 1967.

There were many tall tales told about John Chapman from Longmeadow, Massachusetts. Johnny himself liked nothing better than telling stories of his adventures in the wilderness, stretching the truth just for the fun of spinning a yarn. One tale he loved to tell was about the time his half brother, Nathaniel, came to live with him on French Creek in northwestern Pennsylvania.

When I was still a young man I walked barefoot across the Allegheny Plateau and began planting apple seeds in the wilderness. I sold my seedlings to settlers right there on the frontier. Before long, even if folks had nothing else, they had an orchard. They could eat apples right from their own trees, make apple butter and apple cider, and dry what was left to sustain them in winter. My business prospered, and one day I wrote a letter to my half brother back in Longmeadow, Massachusetts.

Dear Nathaniel,

I am making a comfortable living here on French Creek. There is plenty of work for two and I would welcome your company. Please come soon.

Your half brother,
John

I carried the letter to Mr. Hale's trading post.

Nathaniel rode with the settlers' wagons west to Fort Pitt, and made the last leg of his journey up the Allegheny River from Fort Pitt to French Creek by flatboat. On the way they teased him some.

"I hear tell that your brother John wears a pot for a hat," they'd say, "and just a burlap sack instead of clothes."

Instead of listening to such foolishness, Nathaniel might better have spent his time learning something useful about life in the wilderness.

When he finally arrived on French Creek, I wasn't far off. "You can climb ashore right here, sonny," I heard the boatman shout.

Then I heard Nathaniel ask, "But where's the house and where's my big brother, John?"

"I expect yer big brother is off in the woods someplace discoursin' with squirrels," chuckled the boatman. "And I'll just betcha a pig in a poke that big old hollow sycamore tree is yer new house. Watch out for injuns, sonny," I heard that fool shout as he pushed off, leaving poor Nathaniel alone.

If the boy's ears had worked as well as a boy's ears ought to work, he'd have heard me right there behind him. But when I picked him up and swung him around like a straw scarecrow, he looked as though he'd been snatched up by the spirit world. "Bless you, Nathaniel," I said gently. "Fear no evil, I'm your brother, John. Nowadays folks call me Appleseed John."

I made a fire and boiled some cornmeal into mush. Nathaniel didn't like the look of it, but he gobbled up his share and most of mine like a half-starved mongrel dog.

Then he made himself comfortable inside our cozy sycamore tree. There was a commodious bed of leaves and blankets that I didn't use much, preferring, as I still do, to sleep under the stars.

Over the next days we began gathering nuts and berries. We stored our provisions in hinged boxes to keep friendly critters from helping themselves. We wandered all through the forest, preparing our seedlings to weather the bitter cold.

Autumn ended abruptly that year with an early snowstorm. At first we decorated our camp with snow angels and built ice sentinels along the creek. In the evening I read to Nathaniel and we discussed the great ideas contained in our books. We talked of planting and harvesting apple trees in the spring. At night I slept like a bear.

But Nathaniel soon grew discontented. He huddled inside the sycamore, wrapped in every stitch of warm clothing he had carried from Massachusetts, and munched nuts and dried fruit.

"This isn't exactly what I expected," he complained. "I'm freezing. I wish we had a proper house with a solid door and a stove."

The worst of it was, all his munching soon depleted our stores. Before long we had no more than three fingers' worth of dried fruit and nuts left in the hinged boxes. There wasn't anything to do but risk canoeing downriver to Fort Pitt, where I could purchase enough to feed us both until spring.

"Why can't I come along too?" Nathaniel asked.

"River travel can be dangerous in winter," I explained, wrapping myself in a blanket and pulling a small pot from its peg. "It's much safer here."

"You're not planning to wear that mush pot on your head?" Nathaniel asked.

"Sure am!" I replied. "It's more useful than any hat. It keeps my head dry. I can cook in it, and once I used it to discourage an unreasonable copperhead. Ain't much a man need fear when he's got a mush pot on his head."

I started out paddling rapidly down the half-frozen Allegheny, but big chunks of floating ice made it rough going. Finally, in the late afternoon, I pulled my canoe up on top of a huge cake of ice and stretched out, comfortable as a duke. I closed my eyes for a short nap.

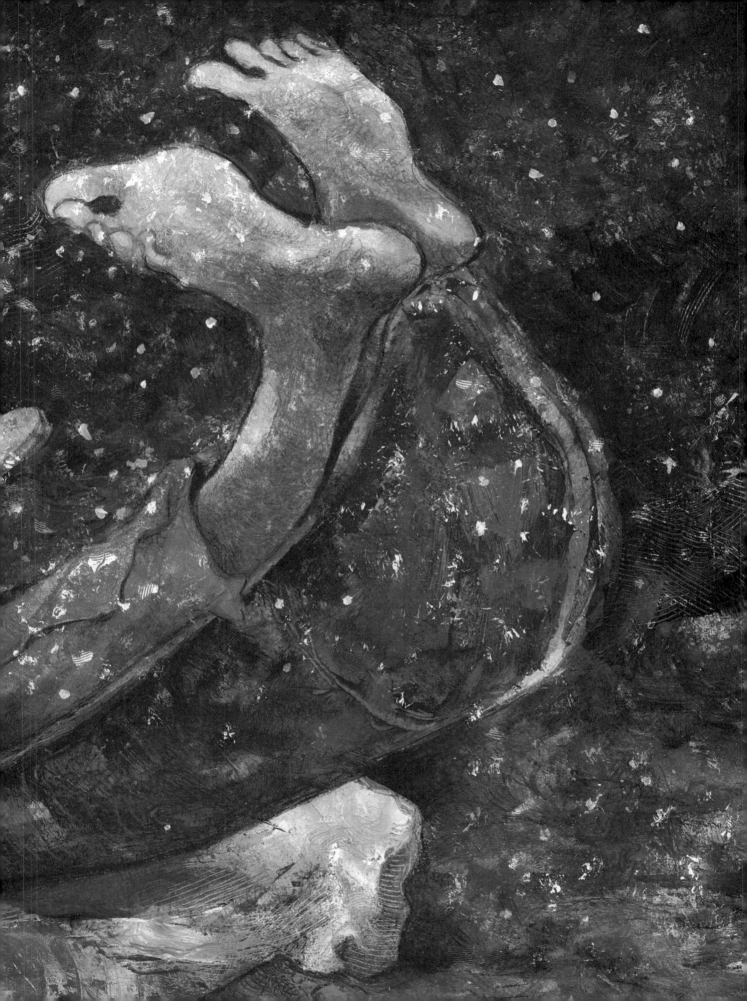

When I felt the morning sun full on my face, I knew right away I must have floated past the fort during the night. A blanket of freshly fallen snow covered me. I made my way to shore, praying that Nathaniel hadn't foolishly gobbled up his meager provisions. But in my heart I was sure that's exactly what he'd done.

I couldn't just paddle back up the icy river, and I was nearly frozen myself. The first thing I needed was shelter. I dragged my canoe up the riverbank. Using it as a windbreak, I made a fire and warmed myself. I wrapped my bare feet with strips torn from my blanket.

Then I waded into the deep snow and cut long, drooping branches from a birch tree. I warmed the branches over the fire until they were soft, and wove them into crude snowshoes. I tied them to my feet with moose bark. Once I had put out the fire and buried my canoe in the underbrush with every intention of returning in the spring, I began the long journey north to where the Allegheny River meets the Monongahela.

When it grew dark I cooked some frozen berries and nuts into mush in my tin pot and slept in a hollow log.

The next day I came upon a lean gray wolf caught in a cruel trap. She regarded me with golden eyes full of hatred and suspicion. I personally have always been on the best of terms with God's wild creatures, and my name, it seems, is widely known among them. "God bless you, madam," I said. "Fear no evil. I'm Appleseed John." Then I gently removed the trap. I tended her through the evening and into the night, washing her wound with snow, and fell asleep to the soft drumming of her heartbeat.

I dreamed of poor Nathaniel shivering in his icy bed. I saw ashes where his fire should have been, and more worrisome still, I saw four braves stealthily creeping toward him along French Creek. I woke with a start, sure that my vision was more than just an ordinary dream. There in the darkness I prayed to the angels. Indians had never done me any harm and I never took anything that belonged to them. But it riled them to see folks settling on their land.

In the morning I trudged on north. My companion limped along beside. We passed several remote cabins. I stopped long enough at the first to ask for something warm to wear. "Any old thing," I said. Those folks had nothing to spare but a moth-eaten old Mother Hubbard. I pulled it over my head gratefully and hurried along through the snow. I guess we made an odd sight, my companion and I. Folks didn't call out or even wave. They just stood, wide-eyed, and watched us pass.

When we reached the clearing beyond the fort, I urged my friend to return to the deep woods, for I feared the soldiers would shoot her.

By the time the sleepy sentry saw me, I was nearly through the gate. "Who goes there!" he kind of squeaked. "Bless you, soldier," I replied. "Fear no evil, I'm Appleseed John." He rubbed his eyes and waved me right on in, though I was ragged and peculiar-looking, and, I expect, smelled worse than a wild pig.

At the general store I purchased beans and blankets, dried fruit and preserves, flour, long woolen underwear, mittens, and even English tea. I found a small bundle of books waiting that I'd ordered from Philadelphia.

I stumbled back through the front gate, past the sentry, and into the snow with enough necessities and comforts to keep us warm and well fed until spring.

"You'd best watch out for injuns, John," a soldier shouted down from the stockade. "There's been talk of trouble up your way."

I shouted back over my shoulder, "Remember that God put us here to be as brothers and sisters and stewards of the earth!"

I soon stumbled upon a muley steer. The beast scraped with his hooves through the snow to the frozen earth and blew a blast of hot steam, like a geyser, from his nostrils. I only narrowly avoided his charge by jumping right out of my snowshoes to a low-hanging branch, leaving my provisions behind in the snow.

"Bless you, sir. Fear no evil," I said, though it was I hanging helplessly overhead. "I'm Appleseed John." Fortunately he had heard of an Appleseed John who found new homes for beasts abandoned in the wilderness. He allowed me to climb down and strap my bundle to his strong back.

That accommodating steer and I plodded north along the river. We kept going through the evening and into the night, past remote cabins with glowing windows. They looked snug and warm, but we didn't slow down or rest until I arrived home.

I saw just what I'd feared, five braves sitting cross-legged around a blazing fire in front of our hollow sycamore tree. One waved his bow wildly in the air, while the others shrieked and whooped. I crept forward, more silently than a snake, hoping to frighten them away and save Nathaniel.

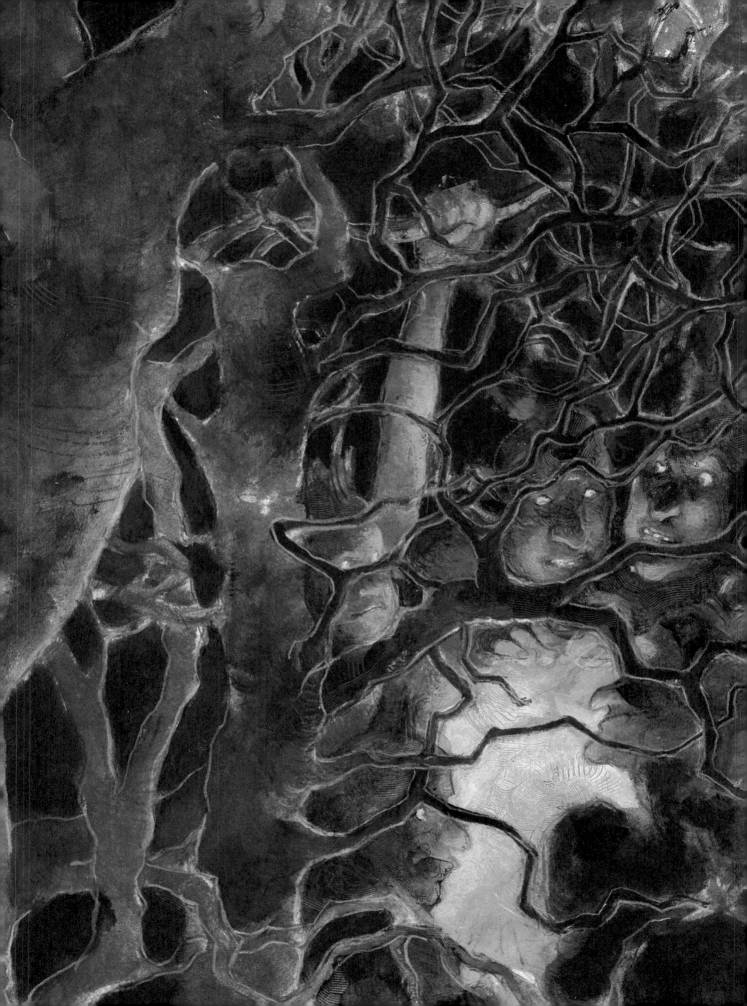

I was all but invisible until I leapt into the firelight, all flapping rags and mush-pot hat.

They jumped to their feet all right, startled, just as if they'd seen a ghost, but instead of fleeing, all five stood their ground. My heart was beating like a war drum. "Bless you all," I said. "Fear no evil." The braves stood silently as stones. My voice trembled. "I'm John."

Appleseed John," they shouted, and laughed and hooted, "we've been waiting for you." Then I recognized Nathaniel. He had feathers in his hair and held a hunting bow. I threw my arms around my little brother and we laughed together.

Young Snake, Bottle Beaver, Twenty Canoes, and Old Halftown turned out to be angels after all. They were Senecas who had found Nathaniel starved and nearly frozen. They had saved his life and taught him to hunt small game with the bow and arrows he made himself. That's their way.

Folks soon came and settled up and down French Creek. Nathaniel stayed on, but I prefer paths through the forest over town roads, so I moved west again, ahead of the settlers, into the Ohio wilderness, carrying a bag filled with apple seeds.

NOTES

This is some of what we know about John Chapman. He was born in Leominster, Massachusetts, on September 26, 1774, in a simple frame house built by his father. The following spring the first shots of the American Revolution were fired at Lexington and Concord. John's father rushed off to join Washington's army. He fought at the Battle of Bunker Hill and served as a carpenter in New York.

When John's mother died in July 1776, he and his sister, Elizabeth, were probably taken care of by relatives. By the time his father returned from the war, John was almost six years old. He and Elizabeth then went to live with their new stepmother in Longmeadow,

Massachusetts. John's father and stepmother had ten more children. They lived together in a little house by the Connecticut River.

John learned to read and write in a public school. But mostly he was self-taught. Years later a false story spread that Johnny Appleseed was a graduate of Harvard University.

When John was ten years old a new wilderness stretching all the way to the Mississippi was opened to settlement. When he was twelve the Northwest Territory was opened.

At a young age John set off by himself, barefoot, it was said, through the mountains across the Allegheny Plateau of northern Pennsylvania. He was caught in an early snowstorm and survived by making snowshoes of beech twigs and moose bark. His destination, the city of Warren, was nothing but a single log cabin on the Allegheny River surrounded by virgin forest. He spent the winter learning every inch of the wilderness up and down the river. In the spring he traveled to the low country along Brokenstraw Creek, cleared some ground, and planted his first orchard.

Farther downriver, about ninety miles north of Pittsburgh, he set up camp at the mouth of French Creek. He was twenty-three years old, five feet nine inches tall, with big hands and feet and either bright blue eyes or, by some reports, dark, almost black-violet eyes.

Senecas and Munsees befriended him. He learned their languages and many of their ways. It was said that he felt at home among them.

It was also widely known that John cared for animals abandoned in the forest, finding them homes or allowing them to live out their lives at one of his many campsites.

In 1801 John moved farther west ahead of settlers and made camp at the mouth of Owl Creek in the wilderness of central Ohio. He began planting trees so that they would be ready to sell by the time the settlers arrived.

John Chapman was a follower and missionary of the Swedish philosopher Emanuel Swedenborg. He carried his philosophy books in a burlap sack. One story is told of John tearing his books into sections and sharing them with remote pioneer families on the frontier, returning later to exchange one section for another and to discuss the section they'd read. He believed this world to be a reflection of the next. It was said he spoke with angels.

Life on the borders of the new frontier was hard. Border folk who opened the new country had to clear out dens of rattlesnakes, fend off wolves, and endure freezing winters with little shelter. John admired the way these people depended on each other, though they were tough and sometimes cruel. Many believed that the only good Indian was a dead Indian. But John told a story of two braves who had come to his camp to warn him of approaching fire and helped him protect his trees. He blamed the settlers for creating most of the trouble because they had cheated and wronged Native Americans.

In the War of 1812, when the tribes of the Ohio Valley, encouraged by the English, tried one last time to drive the settlers from their land, it was said that John took both sides and helped where he could.

After the war John continued to plant and tend his trees throughout Ohio, Pennsylvania, West Virginia, and Indiana. His apple business was successful and he purchased land, though he continued to live a simple, solitary life. In every story he is described as participating in the lives of new families on the frontier. He helped construct their houses and gave seedlings to settlers who could not afford to buy them, and even risked his life to protect theirs in time of danger. At sixty-eight, it was said, he outran forty young men in an attempt to reach a settler's cabin in time to put out a fire.

John Chapman died in Indiana, near Fort Wayne, in March 1845 at the home of a friend.

In time the people of Ashland, Ohio, put up a monument to him. On the stone were engraved the words below.

In telling this story, I chose incidents from John Chapman's life and wove them into a tale, just as he himself might have done.

There is evidence that Nathaniel Chapman lived with his brother on French Creek between 1797 and 1800. A story was told that when his half brother, John, was away obtaining provisions at Fort Pitt, now called Pittsburgh, a band of Senecas and Munsees saved him from exposure and starvation. I chose the Native American names from a list of accounts at Hale's trading post, where John's and Nathaniel's names are also recorded.

In doing my research for the illustrations for this book I traveled to Pittsburgh to see the remains of Fort Pitt, which was formerly known as Fort Duquesne.

A.G.

Johnny Appleseed
Patron saint of American orchards
soldier of peace
he went about doing good.

ABOUT THE AUTHOR

Andrew Glass spent much of his childhood in Westmoreland County, Pennsylvania, not far from French Creek, where this story takes place. He has written and illustrated several books for children, including *The Sweetwater Run: The Story of Buffalo Bill Cody and the Pony Express* and *Bad Guys: True Stories of Legendary Gunslingers . . . of the Wild West.* He has also illustrated many books, including *Soap! Soap! Don't Forget the Soap!* and *She'll Be Comin' Round the Mountain* by Tom Birdseye, and the Spooky Books by Natalie Savage Carlson. He lives in New York City.